This Little Tiger book
belongs to:

_____

_____

_____

For Laura, who is such a brilliant mum ~ SS

For Mum, Dad, Becky, Joe
and S-J with all my love always ~ KH

LITTLE TIGER PRESS LTD,
an imprint of the Little Tiger Group
1 Coda Studios, 189 Munster Road, London SW6 6AW
www.littletiger.co.uk
First published in Great Britain 2020
Text copyright © Stephanie Stansbie 2018
Illustrations copyright © Katy Halford 2018
Stephanie Stansbie and Katy Halford have asserted their rights to be identified as
the author and illustrator of this work under the Copyright, Designs and Patents Act, 1988
A CIP catalogue record for this book is available from the British Library
All rights reserved • ISBN 978-1-78881-731-8
Printed in China • LT/1800/0060/0420
2 4 6 8 10 9 7 5 3 1

My FRiENDS AND ME

Stephanie Stansbie   Katy Halford

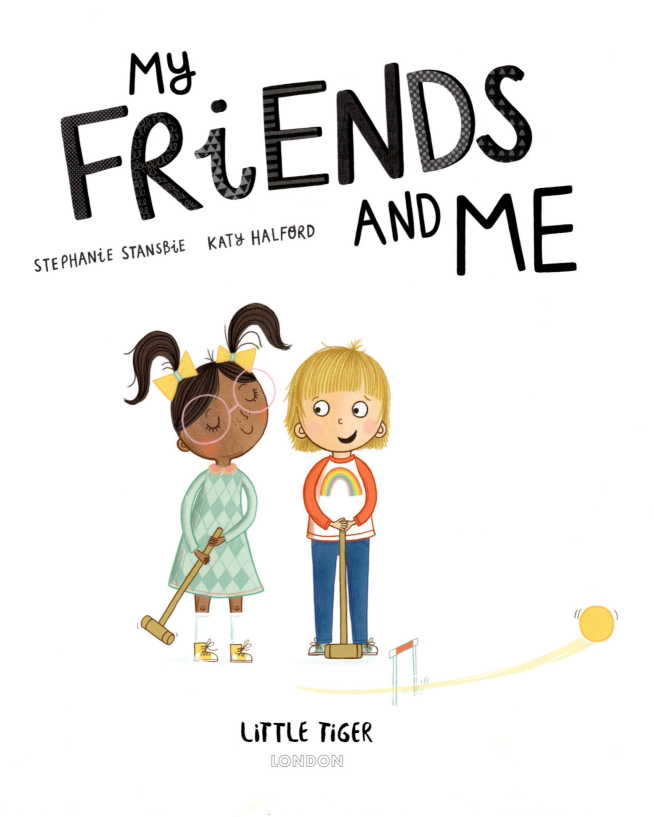

Little Tiger

LONDON

Do you know my mate **Kate**? She's got **two** dads.

Kate's daddy

Frank

They're pretty **cool**, Kate's dads.

They take her out for brunch.

best meal ever!

cute shakers

(In case you're wondering, that's breakfast and lunch all at once.)

cool hair!

My **best** mate Harry has one mum. And she's a **total legend!** Harry's mum is **mega** good at . . .

baking **cakes,**

sword fights

cool moves

Bon-Bon
the bear

and **squishy**

cuddles.

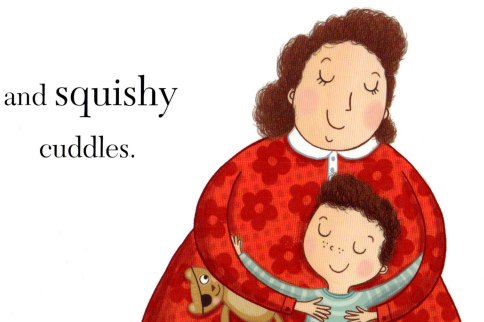

awww!

My friend Olivia has **two** sisters, **two** mums and **one** little brother called Bean.

That's a whole **volleyball** team!

My other pal Lily
is **seriously** lucky.

Lily's
Mum

Oscar

She has **two** houses,

two

wardrobes,

Flo

Madge

Merve

two

beds

and

two

baths!

Lily's dad

Mabel

Lily **always** beats her dad at cards.

(She almost never cheats.)

And her mum lets her stay up really, **really** late!

so past bedtime!

cool fairy mum

My three favourite **sleepover** mates are . . .
Jade (who's got a **massive** house),

real-life
butler!

Jonny (with his cosy caravan)

and Jasper (who lives on an actual boat).

My friend Hannah has a foster mum.

She smells of sweets and is absolutely **brilliant** at juggling.

People used to think Ned's mum was a man.

But it turns out she's a woman.

Ned's mum takes him surfing all the time.

That's pretty awesome – for a grown-up!

primo moves!

But the **coolest** grown-ups
I know are my **granny**
and **grandpops**.

You wouldn't **believe**

the things we get up to!

vrrrooomm!

watch out, chicken!

What I like the **very** most is when we're back at home,
snuggled up and planning a big **party**.

Rose

But the thing with grown-ups is,

it doesn't matter who they are or where they live,

they're brilliant at loving us . . .

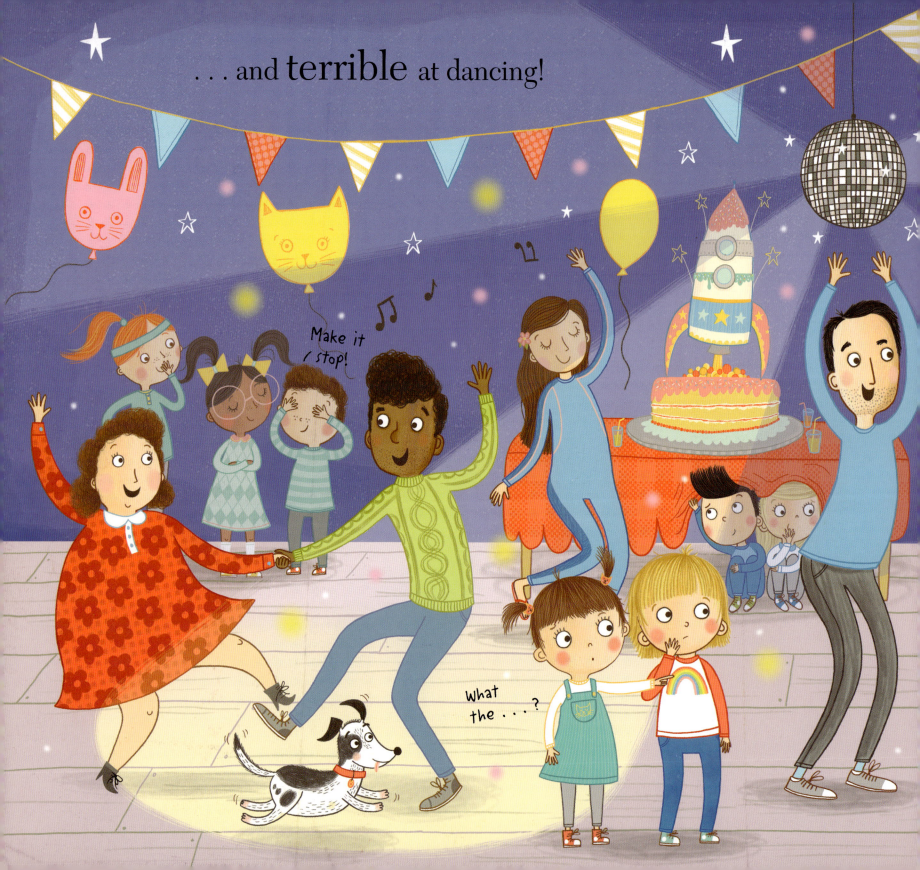

Have a giggle with Little Tiger!

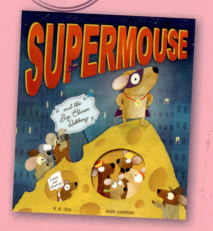

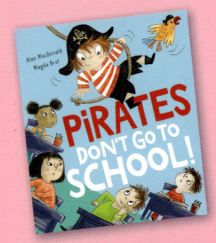

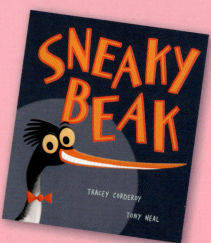

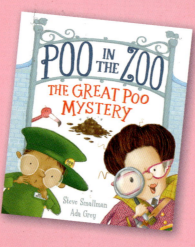

LiTTLE TiGER

For information regarding any of the above titles or for our catalogue,
please contact us: Little Tiger Press Ltd, 1 Coda Studios,
189 Munster Road, London SW6 6AW Tel: 020 7385 6333
E-mail: contact@littletiger.co.uk www.littletiger.co.uk